# Ghost of Willow's Past

a Night Stalkers Christmas short story

by

M L Buchman

**Other works by this author:**
**<u>M.L. Buchman</u>**
The Night Stalkers
*The Night Is Mine*
*I Own the Dawn*
*Daniel's Christmas*
*Wait Until Dark*
*Frank's Independence Day*
*Peter's Christmas*
*Take Over at Midnight*

Angelo's Hearth
*Where Dreams are Born*
*Where Dreams Reside*
*Maria's Christmas Table*
*Where Dreams Unfold*
*Melanie's Independence Day*

*Swap Out!*
*Nara*

Dieties Anonymous
*Cookbook from Hell: Reheated*
*Saviors 101*
*Monk's Maze*

*"And Tomotada looked so long
upon her face it grew rosy red from
chin to forehead, and though she
smiled, her eyes filled with tears."*

*-from "Green Willow" (an ancient
Japanese folk tale of a samurai
who marries the ghost of a willow
tree)*

# 1

**Master Sergeant Dustin James** nudged a clod of dirt back into place with the toe of his boot. The rich black soil of the Portland Oregon Rose Garden simply dissolved and left a blackish patch of mud on the worn leather. Today was the Winter Solstice. It was raining and about three degrees above freezing. Pretty typical. He stared down at the *Rosa canina.*

This rose had been propagated from a cutting of the oldest documented rose bush on the planet. The rose now huddled, dormant and pruned back for the winter. In bloom, it was the least assuming rose in the garden, a single layer of five pink petals around a yellow center. Four days before Christmas, it was a cluster of frosty twigs decorated by bright red rose hips.

Most people passed it by, but not his father, the head gardener of the nearby Japanese Garden. He had visited the rose every day after work on his walk home. Dusty and his mother had often walked up to meet him at the old Briar Rose.

"I met your mother by this rose. We married right here." Being a man of few words, his father never embellished the story. It wasn't the most scenic spot in the garden, but with ten thousand rose bushes in a couple hundred neatly tended beds, not bad either. The fact that they'd married here on the Winter Solstice when nothing bloomed had been a little odd perhaps, but then his parents had been rather eccentric.

Dusty had come home for this Christmas, even though his parents had been gone for three years. Their small condo now lay empty most of the year due to a crashed tourist helicopter. An old Bell 206 called in an engine failure and then auto-rotated right into an Icelandic volcano, no survivors.

That Dusty was a crew chief and me-chanic on a Sikorsky Black Hawk for the U.S. Army's 160th SOAR had made the loss beyond ironic. His job was to fly, fight, and keep the Special Operations Aviation Regiment choppers running perfectly despite war conditions. His parents had died, probably from a broken fan belt.

So, any time that he was home, but especially on the Winter Solstice, he made a point of coming to visit their rose as his parents had done so often for their three decades together.

"I'm glad you went together, at least you got that much," he told the sleeping rose. With no ashes to scatter, he'd gathered some ash from the volcano and scattered it onto the rose's soil. His parents belonged together here. His father, a quiet man who loved visiting the garden's roses, such a contrast to his artistic Japanese garden, and his wild mother, a true child of the sixties, who had never understood Dusty's choice to serve. They appeared such an oddly-matched couple, the slight Eurasian and the tall, busty blonde. "She brings me to life like the spring warmth." "He keeps me steady with his deep roots."

When would Dusty find that? His own dreams had just been pruned back hard. He'd found out, on no notice, that he had a week's leave. He'd rushed back to Portland only to discover that Nancy had meant to Dear Dusty him, but forgotten, as usual, to follow through. Another woman who hadn't understood his need to serve his country, his need to protect that which was so precious. She was living with some software geek named Ralph.

Dusty's few friends still in the area were busy with pre-holiday family stuff. Some invited him over for a meal, but being a third wheel in some other couple's holiday wasn't his first choice, nor his second or third.

On call, Dusty really didn't have time to go anywhere els—

The cry of pain echoing across the garden snapped him out of his damp reverie. His Special Forces training had him sprinting down the garden path before he even fully registered what was happening. One hand slapped for his sidearm, and came away empty. The other slapped for the med kit on his SARVSO survival vest, but he wore only a rain slick over his heavy sweater.

The cry sounded again, a woman in agonizing pain. Halfway across the garden from his parents' rose, he spotted the source. Not that it was hard. On a rainy, winter Friday morning there was only one other person in the garden.

She knelt in the mud at the edge of a garden bed.

Dusty rushed up beside her. "Where are you hurt?" Seeing no obvious wounds he started unzipping her parka.

Her punch came out of nowhere.

She hit him square in the solar plexus so fast he had no time to block it. He tumbled backward among the pruned roses, the thorns carving painful scratches across his cheek and bare hands.

"What the hell are you doing?" the woman shouted down at him. Her hands were poised to strike another blow. He recognized a Taekwondo black belt when he met one and held his hands palm out.

Dusty rolled slowly from the rose bushes onto the wet grass and inspected his hands. "Ow! Shit, that hurts," he flexed a hand and felt every little scratch.

"Answer the damned question!"

He eyed her more carefully. It wasn't your average woman who issued commands to men half-again their size. He blinked the rain from his eyes. She had well-defined cheek bones, arched eyebrows that indicated brunette hair would be hiding under her hood, and eyes the brown of autumn leaves. He shook his head to clear it.

"You sounded like you'd been shot."

"Soldier?" She watched him closely.

"Yes."

She settled back on her heels in perfect balance, clearly poised so that she could attack easily if she decided it was needed.

"Okay. Maybe." She puffed out a breath. "I'm fine."

"You look fine, but you didn't sound it." She did look fine. Not the white of porcelain, but refinement shone in her features. He considered mentioning how much he'd love to draw those features with the artist pencils his mother had given to him as a young child. He didn't know if he'd ever seen so much personality in a woman's features before. It was a face made to laugh and smile, but was now drawn grim and closed.

"I…" In the single word he heard all of the wounded distress return to her voice. She glanced back at the bed of roses she knelt in.

"They cut down the tree," she whispered as softly as the rain.

Dusty looked around, trying to picture this part of the garden in his memory. A tree had been here, a big one.

"It was their willow tree."

That was it.

She pressed the heel of her palm against the center of chest.

"It makes my heart hurt."

2

*Willow saw them in the rain. They reminded Willow of memories grown deep. Though so little remained beneath the soil, the past lay there in Willow's roots. The roses had still been young and new then. Their voices high and nattering. So sure of their beauty, judging themselves in the mirror of human gazes. Silly little things. Willow remembered a Winter Solstice that had been a lifetime ago. Willow knew the two squatting in the rain needed the story. Knowing the cost, Willow reached deep into its remaining roots and prompted the woman to tell the tale.*

# # #

"It was the summer of 1917 when Hiroshi Yamada and Amelia Patterson fell in love. I was named for her." Amy wrapped her cold hands around the large mug of coffee, though it did nothing to warm her hands. She wasn't ready to tell this story, and yet here she was.

Despite her best instincts, the man who had rushed to her rescue had coaxed her out for coffee. Amy had been about to refuse when he'd mentioned her mother's favorite bakery. St. Honore was a neighborhood place, a locals' secret. The *boulangerie* provided a small slice of France in the heart of Portland's oldest residential district.

They sat at the end of the long wooden table, a scattering of croissant crumbs on each of their plates. A couple of guys with laptops sat farther down the table, probably writers, as St. Honore didn't offer wi-fi. Two women, girding themselves with caffeine before picking up kids from kindergarten, occupied a tiny ironwork table crowded among a half dozen similar tables. One hardy soul sat outside at a steel table beneath the awning, turned to shield his book from the occasional gust of rain that spattered against the windows.

"Amelia, my great grandmother, was upper crust Portland Society, a founding member of the Rose Garden. There she met Hiroshi, an assistant gardener for the city. Such a marriage of course wasn't allowed. My great grandmother's diary was kept sealed until she'd been dead for as long as she and Hiroshi had been apart. We actually opened it a year early so that my mother could read it before she died."

Amy's hand shook and she set her coffee down quickly. How had she revealed that her mother died? To a stranger? She hadn't meant to say that. There was no way she was ready to face the loss.

Dusty slid one of his nice hands over hers. She wanted to pull away, but if she did she'd start crying. Actually if she didn't, she'd start as well. There'd been no one to offer her comfort in the last week since her mother's death. She'd been the one offering solace to her mother's friends and facing down bankers and insurance agents and…

She closed her eyes and did her best to close off her feelings. First she had to find her breath, focus not on thoughts but only on what was real, what was physical. From there find her center. From there find the calm.

But when Amy focused on the physical, she felt the warmth and strength of his hand over hers. That warmth drew her attention back off her path and she opened her eyes to look at him.

Dusty wasn't holding her hand, merely resting his over it in comfort. They were working hands, not like hers. No matter what she did, her hands were still long, fine, and delicate. Her mother and her grandmother both had the same hands. People commented on their feminine gracefulness, right before she used them to take the person down in sparring practice.

Dusty was soldier strong—it showed in everything about him—but not some over-built guy. His strong, working-man hands were simply backed up with good shoulders and a trim frame. It was his face that captured her attention. He had beautiful blond hair that rolled down just past his ears, unusual in a soldier. And dark eyes ever so slightly almond shaped.

"What are you?" It didn't come out right. His face was such an odd mix that somehow blended together so wonderfully.

He raised his eyebrows as he sat back and gathered the large porcelain mug into his hands. He didn't appear to take any offense. Nor had he appeared upset when she'd pummeled him into the thorny roses. There was a steady calmness about him that could weather any storm.

Amy missed his comforting hand the moment he withdrew it. *You're feeling way too vulnerable, Amy. Don't do anything stupid.* Her inner-voice guidance system was always wise, so Amy made a practice of following it carefully.

"What am I?" Dusty toyed with the question, again proving he had a great smile. That's how he'd convinced her to join him for coffee, he'd smiled at her. A genuine smile that reached those dark eyes so effortlessly. Amy hadn't realized how starved she'd been for even so simple a gesture.

"I'm my parents' son."

*Shit!* Amy could feel herself closing down again. She no longer had any parents. She needed to go now.

**3**

*Willow waited. Willow knew how to do that.
For as long as the life span of humans, Amelia
and Hiroshi had met each other at Willow.
Hiroshi had planted Willow on a Christmas
Eve while Willow was still a mere shoulder-high
sapling. Willow remembered each of Hiroshi and
Amelia's meetings. In the summer's sun, if they
met, they spoke only with their eyes. But Willow
had waited eagerly for each Christmas Eve, when
the roses' inane chatter had finally settled into
mere winter mumbles. Then Willow watched and
listened and stored those memories in the deepest*

*roots. Willow saw exchanges of small gifts, a kiss, and heard sighs of two hearts broken.*

# # #

"What the hell are you doing here?"

Dusty remained on the park bench under a massive Douglas Fir tree. He had his legs stretched out and crossed at the ankles, his arm stretched across the back of the bench. He'd layered up against the cold day.

He'd hoped Amy might come back to her willow tree, and felt pretty damned pleased with himself he'd been right. It wasn't like he had anything better to do.

"Enjoying the day." He tipped his head back. Yesterday's rain had washed the air clear, leaving the world a breathless blue. The air had a snap to it, his breath made misty clouds that caught the morning sunlight before dissipating.

He'd also enjoyed watching Amy walk down the steps into the garden. The way the woman moved was a thing of beauty. A confidence radiated from her, probably the martial arts training. He could now picture the short, sassy cut of brunette hair beneath the rose-red knit hat. Bet it would shine beautifully in the winter light.

"I wanted to see you again."

The words would probably scare her off, but they were blunt truth, just as his mother had always taught him to speak.

"You left a bit abruptly yesterday."

He'd seen the pain, seen her try to explain. Unable to do so, she'd wrapped her dignity about her like a cloak of steel and lace, thanked him for the coffee, and departed.

He tilted his head. "You're not glaring at me or walking away. I'll take those as good signs."

Amy's slow smile crossed those perfect features and brought yet another aspect of her character to life. He'd decided that if Amy didn't show, he'd probably fly down to Reno and join Chief Warrant Clay

Anderson at the casinos. Even if it didn't inspire him much, it would get him out of Portland.

But now that he'd seen Amy, he canned that plan. Maybe tonight he'd dig around his parents' place and see if he could scare up a sketch pad. He winced against that. Three years and he still thought of the place as theirs. They hadn't left him much in the way of possessions, but the condo was free and clear which gave him somewhere cheap to land on leave. It beat the Army barracks at Fort Campbell hands down. He hadn't even spread out from the small back bedroom he'd grown up in. Maybe he needed to deal with that.

"Dusty?" The smile slipped off her face. He wondered just what his expression had revealed.

"Sorry, I was just thinking. I really need to clean up my place."

"Oh, planning on dragging me back to your den?"

He laughed. He could really get to like this woman. "The thought crossed my mind last night a time or two, but no. It's clean enough. But the condo's still filled with my parents' stuff. I'd be glad to oblige you, by the way."

"Oblige me with what?"

"Dragging you off."

Her sad smile indicated that the answer was "not so much." He hadn't expected more, didn't really know what he was expecting. He'd simply wanted to see more of her; she was also the only other person alone at Christmas he knew in Portland. So he'd come to the garden at sunrise and settled in to watch the day awaken.

"You must be an early riser," he hadn't had to wait very long.

She settled at the far end of the bench, well clear of where his arm draped over the wooden back.

# 4

*Willow listened. Did they know? Would they understand? Stories were like roots, they slide deep under the soil, reaching out and seeking for connection. Willow could feel Amy's heart and how it hurt. Different than Amelia and Hiroshi, but still, hurt. Willow's old roots lay deep under the bench, a whisper beneath the soil.*

# # #

"Still filled with your parents' stuff? Where are they?" Even as she asked, Amy knew.

That grim look clouded Dusty's features, the same as moments before.

She knew the answer and wished she'd never asked, wished she hadn't come this morning. But her mother's ashes were still in her backpack. She hadn't scattered them yesterday because the willow tree was gone. Last night Amy hadn't slept a wink, knowing even if the tree were gone, that spot in the garden was where her mother belonged.

"Mid-Atlantic Ridge, I guess."

Amy squinted at him, but he just shrugged.

"They died in a crash, Icelandic volcano. At least it was quick and they were together which I guess was good for them. I was just thinking that I've never cleaned out their stuff at the condo, because it never mattered. That's just not where they are any more. They're now part of the Mid-Atlantic Ridge, a place where the earth's crust is born."

Amy watched his brows knit together as he looked somewhere far beyond the

Portland Rose Garden. She'd had trouble throwing out the last napkin her mother had used, and here he hadn't cleaned house after three years. She had to be out of the apartment by year end. How in hell was she supposed to do that?

Her mother had hidden her disease from Amy until almost too late. They'd had three days together, most of it spent with her mother in drugged sleep, the rest with Amy reading aloud about Amelia and Hiroshi's yearly meetings at the old willow tree.

It had become a Patterson tradition. Each year since before Amy could remember, they'd come to the Rose Garden and left small presents at the foot of the old willow on Christmas Eve. As a child, Amy had made colored drawings for the tree. Once she'd covered its trunk with little gold and silver star stickers. In later years she'd often purchased a special Christmas ornament to dangle among the bare branches, or scattered a little vial of soil she'd brought back from her travels.

Reading the diary to her mother, they'd finally discovered the origin of the yearly visit tradition. Amy hadn't brought a gift for the tree this year, and with it cut down and gone, she didn't know if she should.

"Sorry," Dusty shook his head like a wet dog. "My mind has gone walkabout."

"I lost my mom five days ago." Again, words she'd never intended to speak had slipped out into the world as if someone had given them a nudge.

Dusty sat bolt upright and turned to her. No longer relaxed back on the bench, his whole attention was on her.

She waited for it, for the words she'd so come to hate. But he didn't speak. He didn't stare at her, though he was looking at her.

Finally she couldn't stand it any longer. "Say it!"

"No. I remember how angry I was at every person who said how sorry they were. It was so empty. Why would I go out of my way to make you angry at me?"

Amy shifted on the cold bench, wishing she'd worn another layer against the chill of the day.

"Who are you?"

His grin was easy. "I guess that's a step up from yesterday's 'What are you?' "

Had she really been so rude? Well, yes, she had.

"Master Sergeant of the 160th SOAR at your service."

"Which battalion?"

That stopped him. Now he really was staring at her.

"The fifth." His voice was now careful.

Amy knew why. SOAR was very secretive. A civilian knowing about the fifth battalion must be unnerving him a bit. She decided to keep her own military background to herself a little longer. She couldn't resist seeing if she could make him squirm. After all, he had stalked her this morning, sort of.

"What do you fly in?"

"DAP." He bit the word off.

The Direct Action Penetrator, the nastiest and most powerful rotorcraft in the world.

"Beale or Henderson?"

"How the hell do you know that?"

"Master Sergeant Amelia Patterson, I flew with Emily Beale in the 101st when she was still a Screaming Eagle. I just finished my five years in the service prerequisite before I could apply to SOAR. I report for testing next week." She held out her hand.

When he didn't respond, she reached out and took his nerveless hand and shook it. Slowly his fingers came to life and curled about hers.

Despite the layers of both of their gloves, she easily remembered the feel of his warm strong fingers covering hers.

He didn't release his hold as they talked.

She didn't try to make him let go though the sun moved far across the sky.

# 5

*Willow listened. It was harder, took more effort. No leaves, no branches, no trunk left. All that now remained of Willow ranged deep beneath the soil. The recent bite of the saw, the tearing of the stump both too painful to recall. But Willow still heard, still felt. He asked the ground to give up its heat and Amy and Dusty talked long through the cold day. It was warm only around that one lone bench in the Rose Garden.*

### # # #

"A friendly face, thank god!" Dusty was deep in packing boxes when Amy dropped by.

"How's it going?"

He surveyed the damage. Bags of clothes for Goodwill lined one side of the living room. Bags of garbage lined the other. Boxes of books to take down to the used counter at Powell's bookstore blocked the couch. He'd kept his father's gardening books and the travel-picture books his mother had collected.

"Okay, I guess. I'm pretty much done. Anything that's too hard, I figure that I'm just not ready to let go of yet. Thankfully, this place is really small, so there aren't too many of those decisions." There'd been hundreds, though it felt like thousands of them, but the passing three years had given him some time to deal with the pain of loss. He'd make sure to offer to help Amy, so that she didn't have to face her mother's past while the wound of loss still bled.

"I've sworn that I'm going to sleep in the big bed tonight, but now I don't know."

He watched Amy as she hung her winter coat on a bronze hook by the door and moved to inspect the progress he'd made. She moved as if this were a military inspection, he followed two steps behind. He could see by her nods that she approved of what he'd kept. Some things she inspected more carefully, those that fit stories he'd told yesterday, others that fit stories not yet told. It was a finely honed and much appreciated assessment. He felt better with each considered nod. Hell, he felt better every single minute they were together.

The master bedroom had a pair of walnut dressers, a small desk, and a queen-size bed with fresh flannel sheets and a faded quilt. Two of his mother's oil paintings of the Rose Garden and a small collection of roses his father had pressed in glass hung on the otherwise bare walls.

She continued her silent inspection and led them into his old bedroom. He'd purged the kid crap long ago. Now it was mostly books and part of his old comic book collection. Some drawings he'd made that his mother had liked enough that he'd pinned them to the wall half a lifetime ago. They weren't half bad, considering.

"Here." She picked up the couple of dinged-up Frisbees he'd kept from his days of playing Ultimate and handed them to him. She also took the two pillows and added that to what he was holding. She moved about the room picking up odds and ends and piling them in his arms.

Then she moved to unpin the art.

"Hey!"

"Shh. It's all right."

He wasn't quite sure how it would be all right, but he subsided and watched as she gently took them down.

She gathered the art carefully, "Okay, let's go."

"Where?" Dusty was feeling a bit dense.

She nodded her head back toward the short hall then led him into his parents' bedroom.

He stood there with his arms full of his old belongings.

"What am I supposed to do?"

She set the art on the foot of the bed. Then she took his parents' pillows and tossed them out into the hall.

"Your pillows go there. The rest is up to you to figure out." She turned back to his old drawings, spread them out across the quilt and then inspected the room's walls.

He started with the pillows. Set some comic books on an empty bookshelf. He dropped his sketch books and drawing pencils on the small desk. He glanced at Amy and then flipped the sketchbook open to a page he'd worked on while unable to sleep most of last night and set it back on the desk.

When he was done she told him to go get his bathroom stuff and move it into the tiny bath off the master bedroom.

After he'd finished, he leaned against the door jamb and watched Amy.

She'd worn jeans and a tight turtleneck that made her a pleasure to watch as she reached to pin each piece of art onto the wall.

He couldn't believe how much he enjoyed this woman. Not her beauty or elegance. Okay, not just her beauty and elegance; she truly had turned his head and his heart completely around. Things he'd avoided for years simply made sense in her presence.

He looked about the room. For the first time in three years it felt right. His mother's art now mixed with his own. Bits of his collection of science fiction and thrillers now leaned against his dad's gardening books.

Amy simply swept him away. The woman was impossible to resist.

Nor did he torture himself by doing so.

He slipped up behind her as she noticed the open sketchbook.

He wrapped his hands around her waist in time to feel the shock of an indrawn breath. He laid a kiss on her neck between her turtleneck and soft hair.

"Is that me?" she whispered.

He nuzzled her neck again and ran his teeth over her earlobe where it just peeked out of her hair. Then he looked down over her shoulder at the charcoal sketch. Her face wasn't drawn from the front. He'd drawn her looking off to the side, as if only just noticing the artist. Her expression reflected a mixture of sadness and the very first hint of a smile. He'd set out to capture her beautiful features, and instead captured her shifting mood. He could still see a woman who had cried at the loss of a tree, but also the woman whose natural state was a quiet joy.

"Best I could do anyway."

"It's wonderful."

"It's a start." He hadn't had as much fun as trying to draw her face in a long time. "You know, I can think of one more thing to help make this room mine."

She turned in his arms and didn't argue as he lay her upon the quilt and began making love to her.

# 6

*Willow rested a little deeper into the dark soil, old roots slowly turning back into the earth itself. But Willow was aware of the bench where Amelia and Hiroshi had kissed and cried each year. And Willow had watched as Amy and Dusty sat, kissing and laughing, the sound trickling into the soil and healing the old pains.*

# # #

Amy had left his bed reluctantly this morning and returned to her apartment to face cleaning out her mother's life. Knowing she was dying, her mother had dealt with most of it, but what remained was still too much. Amy had never felt so helpless.

Half an hour later Dusty had arrived bearing a dozen red roses under one arm, and boxes and garbage bags under the other. He didn't go until all that remained was the cleaning and deciding where to store her own meager belongings. They were all hers now. Maybe she'd ship them to Fort Campbell for lack of anywhere better.

Amy knocked on Dusty's door and waited, ignoring the pleasant tingle running up and down her nerves.

Dusty's invitation hadn't been a casual, "Hey, want to come over for dinner?"

Instead, as he left, he'd slipped a card among the roses. The note had read: "Master Sergeant Dustin James hopes that Master Sergeant Amelia Patterson will join him for a casual Christmas Eve dinner this evening at six." Dustin? Odd that she felt so close to him, had slept with him, and hadn't even known his full name.

The invitation didn't leave her a lot of choice, unless she really wanted to disappoint him. She considered that and decided she didn't want any other choice anyway.

He'd said casual, so, after trying on three different dresses she'd selected dark green slacks and a red silk top. Her hair was too short for her to do anything other than wash it, and she'd never been a fan of makeup. Casual he asked for, casual he'd get.

When he opened the door, she simply stepped into his arms. He turned her just enough to close the door and held her tight. Had she ever found a place she'd been happier than in Dustin's arms? Not a one that she could think of as she breathed in the wonderful smell of him. Man and…

"Is that roast beef?"

"Not mine, though I can cook a mean one. I went down to Elephant Deli. Roast beef and Yorkshire pudding, and a treat for dessert. I did make the peas with those little onions myself."

"From frozen."

"Only the best for Amy."

She laughed and slid back into his arms.

"So, tell me more about your parents' son, Dustin. He strikes me as an interesting chap."

"Well, there was a young boy named Dusty. He had a silent father who loved three things in life: his wife, his son, and his garden." Dusty led her toward the table in the living room. It was now cozy and friendly. While she'd been cleaning her mother's place, he must have been hauling everything out. "And Dusty had a mother who loved laughing."

# 7

*Willow waited. For almost a hundred years, every Christmas Eve someone had come. Willow waited, hoping. Old roots full of broken dreams could do no more.*

### # # #

"Come, walk with me." Dusty held out a hand. He didn't lead her toward the bedroom, where Amy would have followed him happily. He led her to the front door.

"I hope you aren't throwing me out." She slid against him reveling once again in the way their bodies fit together, in the way his lips now tasted of chocolate mousse and winter, the way he lost himself completely in her kiss.

With those strong hands about her waist, he pushed her back just a hand's breadth.

"No way would I throw you out. You're way to precious for that."

"God, don't ever stop saying stuff like that." He made her feel like such a girl, all soft and mushy.

"Deal. But I thought maybe we could go for a walk together."

That knocked the soft and mushy right out of her, but she nodded. Amy braced herself, knowing where they'd go. It was right, but no tree awaited her there. In a fit of sentimentality, she'd bought a small orna-ment that now rested in her coat pocket. Perhaps she'd hang it on one of the roses.

Dusty led her out into the night, up the winding paths beneath the silent Douglas Firs, and around the high, black wrought-iron fence encircling the city reservoir. The light of the full moon lit their breath in billowing clouds and cast brilliant pools on the trail separated by impenetrable shadows. They strolled the back paths leading to the Rose Garden as the silence of the night wrapped gently about them.

For a time they wandered hand in hand between the sleeping rose beds and finally climbed the stairs under the thorny arbors. In the bright moonlight, unbroken by a towering willow, rested the rose bed she'd always thought of as her family's.

"Oh my god!" her voice came out in a cry. "But how?" A slender willow tree, barely taller than she was, stood in the center of the rose bed just where the old willow had.

"I made a call to the Parks Department. My dad worked for them for over thirty years, so I may have thrown his name around a bit along the way. I got permission, and purchased the tree this morning. The master gardener, who my dad trained, came in from vacation and he and I planted it together. I figured, if you wanted, we could come back together in the morning and bury your mom's ashes here on Christmas Day. I already cleared it was okay."

Amy didn't fight the tears that slid hot down her cold cheeks. She wrapped her arms around Dusty and held him and laughed and cried some more.

She pulled the delicate bubble of blown glass from her pocket and hung it from one of the tree's slender branches. There it filled with moonlight and hope and joy.

"It's…" she had to swallow hard to speak. "It's the nicest thing anyone has ever done for me." She could only look at the young tree with its new bauble, for some reason she couldn't turn to look at Dusty.

"Well," Dusty considered Amy's profile and wondered for the hundredth time if he was about to do the stupidest idea he'd ever thought up. Of course that had never stopped him before.

A decade ago, the day before Dusty first reported for basic training, his father had stood with him by the *Rosa canina*, the old Briar Rose. They had stood a long time in comfortable silence, the summer tourists flowing past the two silent men entranced by a single rose bush among ten thousand.

"Your heart knows it is right for you to go into the Army. If you always listen to it, you will make no mistakes, at least not about things that are important."

Dusty heard his heart clearly and knew it was the right choice as he gently turned Amy to face him and he looked down at the tracks of her joyous tears still glistening in the moonlight. He just hoped she thought it was right too.

Again he kissed her long and deep before setting his hands on her waist and stepping her back a half step so that he could form a complete thought.

"Amy?"

"Yes, Dustin?" He liked that she'd started using his full name.

"There's something I have for you that I hope you'll wear some day. It's far too soon, but I know it has to be here, on this night of Christmas Eve, in front of this young willow tree. I hope, Amy Patterson, that someday you'll want to wear this."

He reached into his pocket, then held out his hand before her. In the center of his palm lay the circle of gold with a square-cut diamond he'd chosen that afternoon. It caught the moonlight and glittered.

Amy studied his hand in silence for a long time. She pulled off her right glove and reached out to trace a tentative fingertip once around the circle of gold before withdrawing her hand.

Then she looked up at him, studying him, clearly thinking hard. Maybe he understood his father's silence a little better now, as Dusty found himself struck dumb, mute before this beautiful and amazing woman.

"I think…" Amy's face revealed nothing to him as she inspected his face.

Then that smile flowed across her features as she pulled off her left glove and held her hand out to him.

"I think I'd like to start wearing it now."

# # #

*Young Willow liked the little bubble of blown glass that caught the moonlight, and the reflection of the people past and present. Amelia and Hiroshi. Amy and Dustin. Old pain might run deep, but Young Willow knew, this love would always run as fresh as spring rushing to brighten new leaves, born of the Christmas cold and the moon bright.*

*Young Willow knew that the ghost of Old Willow would agree that they'd done well.*

# End Note

For over ninety years Old Willow (actually a weeping beech which looks like a willow) stood in the heart of the International Rose Test Garden in Portland, Oregon. It was removed for safety reasons in early 2012 and replaced at the turn of the year in 2013 by a young flowering magnolia in the same planting bed (A89). This story lands in the middle of *Wait Until Dark*, the third book in M.L. Buchman's critically-acclaimed "Night Stalkers" series. M.L. Buchman lives and writes in the Pacific Northwest.

# About the Author

**M. L. Buchman, in** among his career as a corporate project manager, has rebuilt and single-handed a fifty-foot sailboat, both flown and jumped out of airplanes, designed and built two houses, and bicycled solo around the world. His romances, as M.L. Buchman, have been named "NPR Top 5 Romance of the Year" and "Booklist Top 10 Romance of the Year." He is now making his living full-time as a writer, living on the Oregon Coast. He is constantly amazed at what you can do with a degree in Geophysics. Please keep up with his writing at www.mlbuchman.com.